The Emperor's New Clothes

By

Hans Christian Andersen

Designed & Illustrated By

Virginia Lee Burton

Houghton Mifflin Co.
Boston

1949

ISBN: 0-395-18415-0 REINFORCED EDITION

ISBN: 0-395-28594-1 PAPERBOUND EDITION

Printed in the United States of America

B&B 20 19 18 17 16 15

With appreciation
to my Father
who shared his enjoyment
of this story with his children

Many years ago there lived an Emperor.

He was so fond of new clothes

that he spent all his time

and all his money

in order to be well dressed.

He did not care about his soldiers
nor did he go to the theatre
or even ride out
except to show off
his beautiful new clothes.
He had a different suit
for every hour of the day.

People would ask, "Where is the Emperor?"
Instead of answering,
"He is in council
with his Ministers,"
his officers would reply,
"The Emperor is changing his clothes
in his dressing room."

Time passed merrily in the big town

which was the Emperor's capital city.

Visitors arrived every day at court
and one day there came two men
who called themselves weavers,
but they were in fact clever robbers.

They pretended that they knew how to weave cloth
of the most beautiful colors
and magnificent patterns.
Moreover, they said,
the clothes woven from this magic cloth
could not be seen by anyone
who was unfit for the office he held
or who was very stupid.
The beautiful clothes could only be seen
by those who were fit for the offices they held
or who were very clever.

"These, indeed, must be splendid clothes!"
thought the Emperor.
"If I had a suit made of this magic cloth,
I could find out at once
what men in my kingdom are not good enough
for the positions they hold,
and I should be able to tell
who are wise and who are foolish.
This stuff must be woven for me immediately."

And he ordered large sums of money
to be given to both the weavers
in order that they might begin their work at once.

So the two men who pretended to be weavers
set up two looms and went on
as though they were working very busily,
though in reality they did nothing at all.
They asked for the most delicate silk
and the purest gold thread.
This they kept for themselves
and put quietly into their knapsacks
and then went on with their pretended work
at the empty looms until far into the night.

After some little time had passed,
the Emperor said to himself,

"I should like to know how the weavers
are getting along with my cloth.
I am a little bit worried
about going myself to look at the cloth
because they said that a fool or a man unfit for his office
would be unable to see the material.
I am sure that I am quite safe
but all the same I think it best
to send someone else first."

All the people throughout the city
had already heard of the wonderful cloth and its magic
and all were anxious to learn how wise or how stupid
their friends and neighbors might be.

"I will send my faithful old Minister
to see how the weavers are getting on with my cloth,"
said the Emperor at last and after some thought.
"He will be the best possible person
to see how the cloth looks for he is a man of sense,
and no one can be more suitable for his office than he is."

So the honest old Minister went into the hall
where the wicked men were working
with all their might at the empty looms.

"What can be the meaning of this?"
thought the old man, opening his eyes very wide.
"I cannot see the least bit of thread on the looms
nor the least bit of cloth woven!"
However, he did not speak his thoughts out loud.

The men who were pretending to weave
asked him very politely
to be so good as to come nearer,
and then, pointing to the empty looms,
asked him whether the design pleased him
and whether the colors were not very beautiful.

The poor old Minister looked and looked
but he could not see anything on the looms
for the very good reason that there was nothing there.
But, of course, he did not know this
and thought only that he must be a foolish man
or unfit for the office of Minister.

"Dear me," he said to himself,
"I must never tell anyone
that I could not see the cloth."

"Well, Sir Minister," said one of the weavers,
still pretending to work.
"You do not say whether or not the stuff pleases you!"
"Oh! It is most beautiful!" said the Minister quickly,
peering at the loom through his spectacles.
"This pattern and the colors!
Yes, I will tell the Emperor without delay
how very wonderful I think them."

"We shall be most grateful to you," said the pretended weavers,
and they named the different colors.
The old Minister listened closely to their fine words
so that he could repeat them to the Emperor,
and then the wicked men asked for more silk and gold,
saying they needed it to finish what they had begun.

Again they were given costly thread and silk
and again they put it all into their knapsacks
and went on pretending to work as busily as before.

The Emperor was pleased with the report
brought by his Minister
and soon after sent another officer of his court
to see how the men were getting on
and to find out how soon the cloth would be ready.

It was, of course, just the same with the officer

as it had been with the Minister.

He looked at the looms on all sides,

but could see nothing at all

but the empty frames.

"Does not the stuff appear as beautiful to you
as it did to my Lord the Minister?" asked the men,
at the same time pointing to the empty looms
and talking of the design and colors
that were not there.

"I certainly am not stupid,"

thought the officer.

"It must be that I am not fit

for the very good comfortable office I have.

That is very odd indeed.

However, no one shall ever know

anything about it."

And at once he turned to the knaves

and praised the material he could not see,

saying he was delighted with both colors and patterns.

He then returned to the Emperor and said,
"Indeed, please your Imperial Majesty,
the cloth which the weavers are making
is extraordinarily magnificent."

The whole city was talking about the splendid cloth

which the Emperor had ordered to be woven at such great cost.

And now at last

The Emperor wished to go himself

and see the marvelous cloth while it was still on the loom.

He took with him a few of the officers of the court,

among whom were the officer and the Minister

who had already seen the cloth

and come back with tales of its beauty.

As soon as the pretended weavers
heard the Emperor coming,
they worked away harder than ever,
though they still did not weave a single thread
through the empty looms.

“Is not the cloth magnificent?”
said the officer and the Minister
who had already seen the weavers’ pretended work.
“If your Majesty will only be so good as to look at it!
What a splendid design! What glorious colors!”
And at the same time they pointed at the empty frames
because they thought that everyone else
could see the wonderful work of the weavers
even if they could not see it themselves.

"How is this?"
said the Emperor to himself,
"I can see nothing! This is indeed terrible!
Am I a stupid man, or am I unfit to be Emperor?
That would be the worst thing
that could happen."

"Oh! The cloth is beautiful," he cried out loud,
"I am delighted with it," and he smiled most charmingly
for on no account would he say that he could not see
what his officer and Minister had praised so much.

All his followers now strained their eyes
hoping to see something in the looms
but they could see no more than the others.
Nevertheless, they all exclaimed,
"Oh, how beautiful!"
and advised His Majesty the Emperor
to have some new clothes made
from this splendid material
and to wear them in the great procession
that was soon to take place.

"Magnificent! Charming! Excellent!"
were said over and over again
and everyone was very gay indeed.
The Emperor pretended to share
in the pleasure of his followers
and presented the two rogues
with the title of Gentlemen Weavers
and the ribbon of an order of Knighthood
to be worn in their buttonholes.

The wicked men sat up all night
before the day
on which the procession
was to take place.
They had sixteen lights burning
so that everyone might see
how eager they were
to finish the Emperor's new clothes.

They pretended to roll the cloth
off the looms.
They cut the air
with their scissors
and sewed with needles
without any thread in them.
"See!" they cried at last,
"The Emperor's new suit is ready!"

And now the Emperor and all his court
came to see the weavers' work;
and the rogues raised their arms
as though they were holding up something to be seen
and said, "Here are your Majesty's trousers!
Here is the scarf! Here is the coat!
The whole suit is as light as a cobweb!"

"When dressed in it one might fancy
that one has on nothing at all.
That, however, is the wonderful thing
about this delicate magic cloth."
"Yes, indeed!" said all the Court
although not one of them
could see anything at all.

"If your Imperial Majesty
would be graciously pleased to take off your clothes,
we will fit on the new suit and undergarments
in front of the mirror."

The Emperor was then undressed,
and the rogues pretended to dress him
in his new clothes,
the Emperor turning round from side to side
in front of the mirror.

"How splendid His Majesty looks
in his new clothes!
And how well they fit!"
everyone cried out.
"What a design! What colors!
They are indeed royal robes!"

"The canopy which is to be carried over your Majesty
in the procession is waiting,"
now said the Chief Master of Ceremonies.

"I am quite ready," answered the Emperor.
"Do my clothes fit well?" asked he,
turning himself around again
in front of the mirror
in order that he might look as though
he were admiring his handsome suit.

The Lords of the Bedchamber
who were to carry His Majesty's train
felt about on the ground
as if they were lifting up the ends
and then pretended to be carrying something.
They could never for a moment
let anyone think that they were stupid
or unfit for their office.

So now the Emperor walked under his high canopy
in the middle of the procession
right through the streets of his capital city.
And all the people standing by
and those at the windows cried out,

"Oh, how beautiful are our Emperor's new clothes!
What a magnificent train! And how gracefully the scarf hangs!"
In fact, no one would admit that he could not see these clothes
which everyone seemed to think so beautiful
for fear he would be called a simpleton or unfit for his office.

Never before had any of the Emperor's clothes caused so much excitement as these.

"But the Emperor has nothing on at all!!!"

said a little child.

"The child tells the truth," said the father.

And so it was that what the child said

was whispered from one to another

until all knew

and they cried out altogether,

"BUT HE HAS NOTHING ON AT ALL!!!"

The Emperor felt very silly

for he knew that the people were right

but he thought, "The procession has started

and it must go on now!"

So the Lords of the Bedchamber

held their heads higher than ever

and took greater trouble to pretend

to hold up the train which wasn't there at all.

THE END